The Magic of Pomme

Story by Ilse Sondheimer   Pictures by dee deRosa

For Lillian M. Feldman

RAINBOW PRESS
222 Edwards Drive
Fayetteville, N.Y. 13066

1 2 3 4 5 6 7 8 9 10 11 12

Kati liked getting things done.

Once, when a foolish black kitten climbed on the roof of the barn and meowed sadly because it couldn't get down, Kati asked two of the bigger children to hoist her up until she could get hold of the ladder. She climbed to the peak and slid on her belly until she could reach that foolish kitten and bring it down safely.

Another day Kati saw that it was starting to rain. Quickly she dragged a stool into the yard so that she could reach the clothesline. Just as soon as she had taken that first snowy white sheet off the line, the wind came along and rushed it out of her hands. She had to chase that sheet down the cowpath, and didn't catch up with it until it landed on a neighbor's fence.

Kati lived in the village of Pomme where almost every family had an apple orchard. The apples that grew there tasted sweet and sour at the same time. They were firm, and they were bigger than any other apples in the land.

In the fall people came from many miles away to buy the apples. They bought cider which was sweet and sour too, and pies and cobblers which were rich and moist. And they bought honey which the bees had made from nectar they took from the apple blossoms in the spring.

It was told throughout the land that more than good things to eat came from the apples which grew in Pomme.

The people who came to Pomme to buy the apples and cider and cobblers often took the bridge across the river. They liked looking at the graceful arches of the bridge, and they liked talking to their children about other wonderful things to be found in Pomme.

"The people who live there are lucky," one father said. "They are lucky because every year, in the fall, one of their children eats an apple which turns out to be a magic apple. Even though it looks and tastes no different from any other, the child who eats that apple can then do something that is very special."

"And such is the strength of the magic in that apple," the mother added,"that anyone who spends time with the child who has eaten it, might then do something that is special too. Some people in Pomme have built handsome houses, and some have made wonderfully comfortable shoes of beautiful soft leather. Others have written stories and poems and songs, and still others have made up new recipes for pies and cobblers."

"And brothers and sisters have been known to spend days together without fighting and teasing."

Kati had eaten lots of apples, but not one of them had been magic. There were many stories about children who had found a magic apple, and Kati quite believed that each of these stories was true. There was the story about Amanda who liked munching an apple while she walked by herself in the meadow. She came back from one of her walks and said to her folks:

"Do you want to hear a song?"

She sang a song that no one had ever heard before, and she sang so well that the neighbors all came to listen.

Then there was a story about a small boy whose name was Jonathan. Right after eating one of the tart, green apples, he made up a very scary story and told it to his friends.

"Tell it again!"
one of the children said, as soon as Jonathan was finished.

Another story Kati liked was about Marcia.

Marcia ate a bright, golden apple, and then painted a picture that was so beautiful that anyone who looked at it felt good all the rest of that day.

Kati liked watching Marcia sketch and paint.

One day Kati drew a picture of the colt, her grandfather's favorite horse.
Her grandfather said: "That's a fine picture, Kati!"
But Kati knew that it would not make him feel good all the rest of that day.
Kati liked drawing. Her next picture was of the mare, the brown colt's mother.

Grandfather hung both pictures in his parlor.

In the wintertime people worked

on new recipes   on poems and songs   and on making comfortable shoes.

Before the winter was over they pruned their apple trees.

Until the year of the big rain.

  That year it rained in the spring, and it rained in the summer. The roads were muddy and the fields were flooded. The river water rose higher and higher, and finally, the bridge with the graceful arches was washed away.

    In the spring the few apple blossoms on the trees were blown away by the wind before the bees could do their work. In the fall there were no apples. The people who came from many miles away all went back home without spending their money in Pomme.

    Oh, it was bad!

Men and women who used to make up songs and poems and stories and new recipes now watched the rain come down. There was no money for new roofs, and many rooms had raindrops dripping into buckets.

Kati listened to the grown-ups talk.

"Even if we get apples again next year, people won't come if they can't come across the bridge," said one.

"Even if we build a new bridge, another big rain might wash it out," said somebody else.

Marcia told Kati that she and her family would have to move away.

"Why?" Kati wanted to know.

"Because nobody has money to buy my father's shoes." Kati went home and told her mother.

"I know," said Kati's mother, "we may have to move too. There's just no money to be earned in Pomme."

"Where will we go?" asked Kati.

"We'll move to the city. There are jobs to be found there."

"Will Grandpa go with us?"

Kati's mother shook her head. "No."

Often now children were sent to bed without being told a bedtime story. Kati missed stories as much as she missed good things to eat.

One evening Kati was in her bed thinking about the things that used to be. She started to cry, and because she could not think of one thing that she could do about having to move, she cried some more—until she fell asleep.

Early the next morning Kati went to see her grandfather.

"I'm down here," he called from the cellar, "careful on those stairs."

Kati couldn't believe her eyes. There was a great big pile of dirt in the middle of the floor, and Grandpa was adding to it from the side where there was a hole in the wall.

"What are you doing, Grandpa?"

He went on shovelling.

"I'm building an apple room."

"But Grandpa, there aren't any more apples."

"Next year, there will be apples again. Then I'll store them here, where they'll stay cold, but they won't freeze. And they'll taste good in the winter, and in the spring, and even through the next summer." Kati looked at the big pile of dirt.

"But what about the magic apple?" she asked softly, "could I still find it, down here?"

"Yes, Kati, I think you could. But magic is more apt to happen when you do something to get ready for it."

Kati was very quiet all that day. At night she was in her bed, but this time she was not crying. When the moon came out and looked through Kati's window, she whispered, "I'll do it now!"

Quickly she got up. Barefoot, and in her nighty, she slipped out of the house.

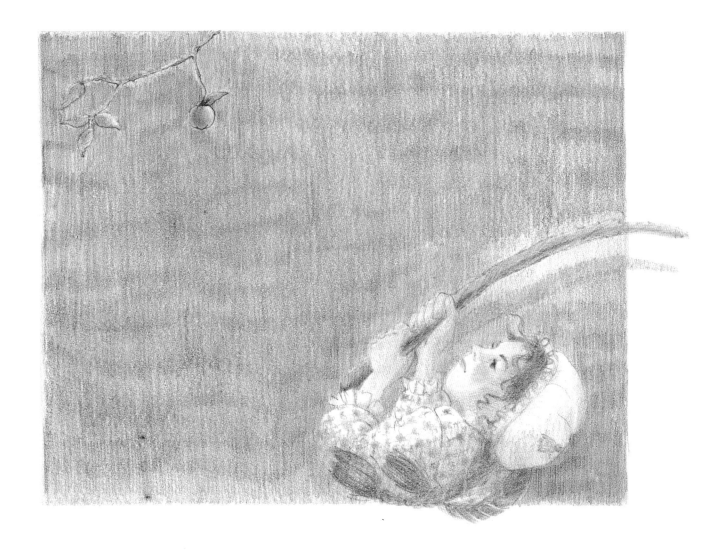

She followed the path to the orchard and looked up at the black and shivering trees. She walked between the rows until she saw a tree that had one small apple still clinging to a branch. She couldn't reach the apple, but she found a sturdy stick and used that to hit at the branch. Again and again she hit it until the apple fell down.

It was small and shrivelled, but she picked it up and quickly ran home with it. In her room Kati bit into the soft brown apple. It wasn't sweet, and it wasn't sour, but, except for the core, Kati ate every bit of it.

Then she got to work. No one knows how long Kati stayed up that night, but before going back to bed she finished drawing a picture of the bridge with the graceful arches—as it had looked before the rain had washed it out.

In the morning Kati's mother and father saw the small apple core, and they saw the picture. They called the neighbors to come over and see it too.

"Oh, it was a grand bridge!" said one of the men.

"Yes," said his wife, "nobody could build a more beautiful bridge."

"That's true," said a young man, speaking slowly, "nobody could make it more beautiful, but it could be made stronger."

For a moment no one said anything. And then they all seemed to have something to say at the same time.

"The piers would have to go down deeper, through the mud and the sand, and into the rock."

"We would need everybody to help us work on it. Do you think that they will stay?"

"Yes," said Kati's grandfather, "I think they'll stay, as long as they know that they are doing something that will help."

And so the men and women, the girls and boys, all worked together to build a new bridge.

When the bridge was finished people started to come again from many miles away.

To this day they talk about how beautiful the bridge is, and how strong.
And they tell their children about the luck of the village of Pomme to have a magic apple growing there, year after year.

And before going back home, there are some who fill their baskets with apples, and their casks with cider; and then they knock at the door of Kati's house and ask to see her picture.

The illustrations for this book were done
with colored pencils on Bristol board.
The text type was set in 14 pt Palatino.
The book was printed by Midstate Printing
Corporation in Syracuse, NY.
Production supervision by Ilse Sondheimer.
Book design by dee deRosa .